Angelina in the Wings

Published by Pleasant Company Publications
First published in Great Britain by Penguin Books Ltd., 2002
© 2002 HIT Entertainment PLC
Based on the text by Katharine Holabird and the illustrations by Helen Craig
From the script by Barbara Slade

Visit our Web site at **www.americangirl.com** and Angelina's
very own site at **www.angelinaballerina.com**

Printed in Hong Kong

02 03 04 05 06 07 08 09 C&C 10 9 8 7 6 5 4 3 2 1

Angelina™
Ballerina™

Angelina in the Wings

PLEASANT
COMPANY
PUBLICATIONS™

"I have wonderful news!" said Miss Lilly one day after class. "As you know, the famous Madame Zizi is to perform *The Sun Queen* at the Theater Royal. And she is coming here tomorrow with Mr. Popoff, the director, to watch our class!"

Everyone gasped with delight.

"One of the little sunbeams in the ballet has mousepox," Miss Lilly continued.

"Does that mean they need another sunbeam?" asked Angelina, hardly daring to believe it.

"It does, Angelina! Indeed it does," said Miss Lilly with a smile.

That evening at supper, Cousin Henry was running around the kitchen, playing with his windup ladybug and singing. He was very excited about Angelina being a sunbeam.

Angelina, however, was getting nervous. "Don't worry," said Mrs. Mouseling. "You'll have Henry there as your mascot!"

"WHAT!" Angelina was horrified. "I have to take Henry to the audition?"

"I'll be the best mascot ever!" said Henry, spilling his drink.
"What's a mascot?"

"Someone who brings luck," said Mrs. Mouseling cheerfully.

Angelina groaned.

The next day at class, Angelina felt very nervous.
Mr. Popoff was going to teach the lesson so that
Madame Zizi could watch the mouselings dance.
Henry sat at the side of the room, playing with his
ladybug and trying to keep still.

"Alice!" whispered Angelina to her best friend as they
began to dance. "This sunbeam is about to shine!"

As Angelina spun around the room, she hissed at Henry to sit quietly.

"Zee leetle peenk mouseling," said Madame Zizi suddenly.

"On your own, please," said Mr. Popoff.

"Enchantee!" exclaimed Madame Zizi, as she watched Angelina dance on her own.

Suddenly a fly landed on Henry's nose, and he dropped his ladybug. "Oh, no!" he cried, chasing his toy across the floor. The ladybug bumped into Angelina, and over she toppled.

"What a sweet mouseling!" said Madame Zizi, spotting Henry. "He must be our sunbeam! Zee peenk one can understudy."

"I can't believe Henry got the part!" sobbed Angelina that evening. "And I just have to stand and watch. It's so unfair!"

Alice tried to comfort her. "But when Madame Zizi sees how good you are, she's bound to make room for another sunbeam!" she said cheerily, offering Angelina a cheesy niblet.

The next day, all the sunbeams, and Angelina, danced in perfect time. Except for Henry.

"Jump like Angelina!" said Mr. Popoff.

Henry tried hard, but it was very difficult for such a tiny mouse.

"Move back, Angelina!" continued Mr. Popoff. "They must do it alone."

That evening, Angelina called Alice. "How can I get Madame Zizi to notice me?" she cried desperately.

She watched little Henry as he danced around the room. Mrs. Mouseling came in just as he tripped over Angelina's ballet things, thrown carelessly on the floor. "Oh, Angelina! I'm not your servant!" Mrs. Mouseling scolded as she began picking things up.

Servant! thought Angelina. That's a good idea!

The next day, Angelina did everything for Madame Zizi.
She ran around fetching and carrying until she was
exhausted. Just before the rehearsal, she even helped
with Madame Zizi's costume!

"Where is the little boy mouseling?" asked Mr. Popoff impatiently a few minutes later. "We are ready to start!" Everyone looked around.

"Here I am!" sang Henry, running onto the stage a little out of breath. He'd gotten lost backstage.

Madame Zizi swept him into her arms. "Eet is not hees fault," she said. "Angelina should have been looking after heem like I told her to!"

As she waited backstage, Angelina began to sob.
Alice tried to cheer her up.

Then Angelina and Alice heard Mr. Popoff's voice coming from the stage. "Zizi, we have to bring on the understudy sunbeam! The boy mouseling must go!" Angelina was stunned. Poor Henry!

"Please give him another chance," Angelina cried. "I can help him. I promise!"

Madame Zizi agreed. "Yes, Popoff! You weel geev heem one more chance at the dress rehearsal tomorrow. I inseest!"

That evening, Angelina helped Henry as he struggled
with the difficult steps. "Well done!" she said. "Now
we'll try it again. Watch me!"

At last it was time for the dress rehearsal. At the theater, the sunbeams waited in their dressing room with Mr. Popoff, ready to go onstage.

Suddenly, Madame Zizi rushed in.

"Whatever is the matter, Zizi?" asked Mr. Popoff nervously.

"Disaster!" she replied. "Another one of our leetle sunbeams has zee mousepox!"

Angelina had her chance at last! The little sunbeams danced their hearts out, and at the end of the performance, they took their bows behind the famous Madame Zizi.

As the performers left the stage, the applause was deafening. Mr. and Mrs. Mouseling, Henry's parents, Alice, and Miss Lilly leaped to their feet and clapped as hard as they could.

"Oh, Henry! You were wonderful," said Angelina breathlessly.

"You were indeed perfect, Henry," said Mr. Popoff with a smile. "And it was all thanks to you, Angelina!"

The next morning, Angelina and Henry sat side by side in bed, covered in pink mousepox spots! They heard a knock on the bedroom door.

"Room service," laughed Mrs. Mouseling, popping her head around the door. "I've brought some cheesy niblets, sent by Alice, for two spectacular spotty sunbeams!"

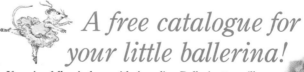

American Girl ®

PO BOX 620497
MIDDLETON WI 53562-0497

‖‖‖

┃┃┃┃╻┃┃┃┃┃┃┃┃┃┃┃┃┃┃┃┃┃┃┃┃┃┃┃┃┃┃┃┃┃┃┃┃┃┃